Published in the United States of America by The Child's World®
1980 Lookout Drive • Mankato, MN 56003-1705
800-599-READ • www.childsworld.com

ACKNOWLEDGMENTS
The Child's World®: Mary Berendes, Publishing Director
The Design Lab: Kathleen Petelinsek, Design and Page Production
Literacy Consultants: Cecilia Minden, PhD, and Joanne Meier, PhD

LIBRARY OF CONGRESS
CATALOGING-IN-PUBLICATION DATA
Moncure, Jane Belk.
  My "f" sound box / by Jane Belk Moncure ;
illustrated by Rebecca Thornburgh.
    p. cm. — (Sound box books)
  Summary: "Little f has an adventure with items beginning with
her letter's sound, such as four fish, five fat frogs, and a funny
fox"—Provided by publisher.
  ISBN 978-1-60253-146-8 (library bound : alk. paper)
  [1. Alphabet.] I. Thornburgh, Rebecca McKillip, ill. II. Title. III.
Series.
  PZ7.M739Myf 2009
  [E]—dc22   2008033162

A NOTE TO PARENTS AND EDUCATORS:

Magic moon machines and five fat frogs are just a few of the fun things you can share with children by reading books with them. Reading aloud helps children in so many ways! It introduces them to new words, motivates them to develop their own reading skills, and expands their attention span and listening abilities. So it's important to find time each day to share a book or two . . . or three!

As you read with young children, you can help develop their understanding of how print works by talking about the parts of the book—the cover, the title, the illustrations, and the words that tell the story. As you read, use your finger to point to each word, modeling a gentle sweep from left to right.

Simple word games help develop important prereading skills, including an understanding of rhyme and alliteration (when words share the same beginning sound, such as "six" and "sand"). Try playing with words from a book you've just shared: "What other words start with the same sound as moon?" "Cat and hat, do those words rhyme?" The possibilities are endless—and so are the rewards!

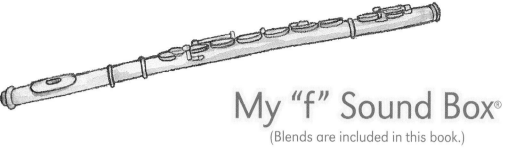

My "f" Sound Box®

(Blends are included in this book.)

WRITTEN BY JANE BELK MONCURE

ILLUSTRATED BY REBECCA THORNBURGH

Little  had a box. "I will

find things that begin with my

f sound," she said. "I will put

them into my sound box."

Little  found a fishing pole.

She caught four fish. Did she put the fishing pole and the four fish into her box? She did.

Then she caught five fat frogs.

Did she put the five fat frogs

into the box with the fishing pole

and the four fish? She did.

Little  walked through a

forest of fir trees.

She put a fir tree into her box.

"I will leave the other fir trees in  the forest," she said.

Suddenly, she saw a fox. It was

a funny fox!

"I will put this funny fox into my

box," said Little  .

"What funny things I have in  my box! I have a fishing pole, four fish, five frogs, a fir tree, and a fox!"

Little 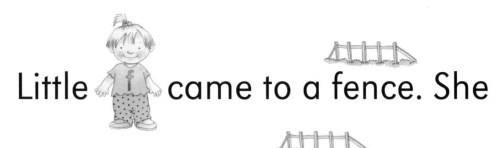 came to a fence. She

climbed over the fence and saw

a field of flowers.

She filled her box with flowers.

Then Little  saw a farmhouse.

The farmer ran from

the farmhouse.

"Fire!" he cried. "The farmhouse

is on fire! Help!"

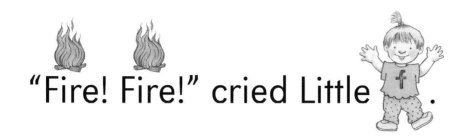

"Fire! Fire!" cried Little .

She ran back through the field of

 flowers, over the fence, through the

 fir forest, and all the way to the

fire station.

"Fire! Fire! Fire!" she shouted.

"The farmhouse is on fire!" She

rang the  fire alarm.

Five  firefighters jumped onto a fire truck. Little jumped on, too.

They gave Little  a fire hose

and a firefighter's hat. They gave

her boots and a firefighter's coat.

The fire truck went fast.

The  firefighters put out the

fire.

"Thank you," said the  farmer.

"Thank Little ," said the five firefighters. "She is our friend."

Then the  firefighters took Little f and her box back to the fire station.

Little  opened her box.

She took out her funny things.

Everyone played!

My, what fun they had!

Little  f 's Word List

farmer

farmhouse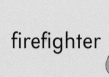

fence

field

fire

fire alarm

firefighter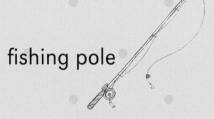

fire hose

fire station

fire truck

fir tree

fish

fishing pole

flower

forest

fox

friend

frog

28

Other Words with Little

fan

feather

feet

finger

fingers

flag

flamingo

flashlight

flute

fly

foot

football

fork

french fries

fruit

29

More to Do!

Little  rang the fire alarm and saved the farmhouse. You can create a book of fire-safety tips for you and your family.

What you need:

- 2 pieces of stiff paper or construction paper
- up to 6 sheets of regular paper
- pencils, markers, and crayons
- a hole punch
- a shoestring

Directions:

1. Draw a cover for your book on one of the stiff pieces of paper. Make a colorful back cover using the other piece of stiff paper. Set these aside.

2. Choose some (or all) of the fire-safety tips below. Have an adult write one tip across the bottom of each piece of paper.

   - Check the batteries in your smoke alarms.
   - Keep a fire extinguisher in your kitchen and garage.
   - Have a family exit plan in case of a fire. Practice the plan once a month.
   - Visit a nearby fire department to learn more about fire safety.
   - Always put out your campfires.
   - Never play with matches.

3. Use your markers and crayons to draw the safety tip listed at the bottom of each piece of paper.

4. Stack your papers in the order in which you want them to appear in your book. Put the front cover on top of the stack. Put the back cover on the bottom—but be sure the side you drew on is facing down!

5. Use a hole punch to put two holes along the left side of all the papers. Loop the shoestring through the holes and then tie a bow. Now you have a good book for the whole family to read!

About the Author

Best-selling author Jane Belk Moncure has written over 300 books throughout her teaching and writing career. After earning a Master's degree in Early Childhood Education from Columbia University, she became one of the pioneers in that field. In 1956, she helped form the Virginia Association for Early Childhood Education, which established the first statewide standards for teachers of young children.

Inspired by her work in the classroom, Mrs. Moncure's books have become standards in primary education, and her name is recognized across the country. Her success is reflected not only in her books' popularity with parents, children, and educators, but also by numerous awards, including the 1984 C. S. Lewis Gold Medal Award.

About the Illustrator

Rebecca Thornburgh lives in a pleasantly spooky old house in Philadelphia. If she's not at her drawing table, she's reading—or singing with her band, called Reckless Amateurs. Rebecca has one husband, two daughters, and two silly dogs.